Single
GIRL RULES
#BFF

USA TODAY BESTSELLING AUTHOR
IVY SMOAK

This book is a work of fiction. Names, characters, places, and incidents are fictitious. Any resemblance to actual persons, living or dead, events, or locales is purely coincidental.

ISBN: 9798478539153

2021 First Edition

Single Girl Rule #1
Boys are replaceable. Friends are forever.

Prologue

RUNAWAY BRIDE
Saturday - Oct 10, 2026

The hairdresser stepped back to admire her work. "What do you think?"

After hours of sitting around in curlers and drinking mimosas...I was feeling more than a little buzzed. I thought I looked damn good. But before I could answer her, my wedding planner, Justin, strutted into the room.

He took one look at me and smiled. "Chastity, you are the picture of perfection."

"Yeah, bitch, I know."

He laughed. "Pictures start in thirty minutes. We need to get you into your dress. And where is Ash?"

"In here," Ash said from the adjoining restroom.

"Well, come out," Justin said. "We need to make sure it fits okay. Time is ticking, ladies!"

Ash groaned and stepped out in her hideous bridesmaid dress.

I couldn't help but laugh. It was truly awful. I didn't even want such a monstrosity in my wedding pictures. But payback was a bitch. And you should have seen what she'd made me wear at her first wedding. That sly whore tried to make up for it at her second wedding, but we were still not even.

"That dress is…fitted," Justin said. It was pretty much the only nice thing to say. It was freaking terrible. But it did fit her well.

"Stop laughing at me," Ash said and glared at me. "I'm going to kill you."

I shook my head. "You say that to me all the time. And yet…here I am alive and well on my wedding day!" I lifted my champagne glass in the air. "Ah, I'm getting married!" I stood up and wobbled a little in my heels. *Definitely too many mimosas.* I quickly downed the one in my hand and handed it to my hairdresser.

"Come over here," I said and grabbed Ash. "We need a picture right now."

"I've got you," Justin said. He snapped a picture of Ash looking terrible and me looking like a queen in my satin robe and high heels. God, this really was the best day of my life.

Justin and Ash worked together to get me into my dress.

"I can't believe I'm actually getting married," I said and stared into the mirror. Ash's dress was a taffeta nightmare. But my wedding dress was more of a dream. Actually, that was almost exactly what I said when I'd first put it on. *A risqué dream.* The v-neckline dipped way too low. And there were way too many sheer parts. And it was way too tight. Way too everything. Or at least…that was what everyone told me. They were totes wrong, though. It was perfect. And it was so easy to picture the layers spread out all around me on the floor as I sat on my soon-to-be husband's face tonight. That's right - he was a giver.

"You look simply radiant," Justin said.

Ash sniffled. "You really do. You're the most beautiful bride ever."

"Don't cry!" I said. "You're going to make me cry!"

"No one cry!" Justin snapped. "I swear if I see one tear I'm going to make you get all your makeup redone. We will have no tearstained cheeks in these photos, people!" The walkie-talkie on his hip started going off. "Wedding planner duties are calling! Don't smudge your makeup, or I swear to God…"

Chastity laughed as Justin ran out of the room.

Ash sighed. "I'm so happy for you. And your fiancé is going to die when he sees you walk down the aisle. You two are perfect together."

We really were. He was every dream of mine come true. I wouldn't just give up the single girl life for anyone. "Oh my God." I grabbed Ash's arm.

"What? Are you okay?"

"No! The Single Girl Rules!"

Ash just stared at me. "Right. I'm so glad you're going to be done with those. Goodbye and good riddance."

"No!"

"No what? You're going to be married. You can't do that crazy stuff anymore. It's completely inappropriate."

"I know that. I meant 'no' as in *fucking no*! How could I forget? I've been so busy with last-minute wedding details that I didn't give the rules back! This is a disaster! We need to leave right this second!"

"Um…" Ash stared at me in my wedding dress. "Chasity, we can't go anywhere. We're taking pictures before the ceremony. We're supposed to be out in the gardens in like half an hour."

"Did you not hear what I just said? This is an emergency! A 911 situation. I have to put the Single Girl Rules back right freaking now." I lifted the hem of my dress, ready to make a run for it.

"Back where? Cut it out, Chastity. We both know you made up those rules."

"I did not! How many times do I have to tell you this? The rules came to me when I needed them most, and now I have to put them back for someone else to find. Come on." I grabbed Ash's hand and pulled her out of the wedding suite.

"Slow down!" called Ash. "I can't run in these stupid shoes."

Her shoes were as dumb as her dress. But she should have thought about that when she'd made me wear one-inch pumps to her first wedding. One-inch. What was I...80 years old? I'd paid her back by giving her six-inch heels because she was bad at walking in them. I loved being a bridezilla. It suited me.

I pulled her down a hallway and put my back against a wall so no one could see us.

"What are you doing?"

"Shh!" I hissed. "We're making a getaway."

"Oh. So you are having cold feet? I get it. I'm a little relieved. I know I said you two were perfect for each other, but he is a little weird."

"Excuse you? I'm not having cold feet. I'm going back to college." I slowly peered around the corner to see if the coast was clear.

"I'm pretty sure that's cold feet. And we can't go to Newark right now. We'll miss the whole wedding. It's over a two-hour drive…"

"That's why we're taking my perfect soon-to-be husband's helicopter. Now stop saying insane stuff and let's make a run for it!" *Okay, fine.* I know I sounded insane. But this was important. I wasn't going to be a single girl anymore. And it went against the whole principle of the Single Girl Rules to hoard them from other single girls.

I grabbed Ash's hand and we made a run for it. We made it out of the mansion and into the gardens without being spotted. Everyone else was still either getting ready or setting up for the ceremony inside. It was the perfect getaway.

Or not. Because Justin had just burst out the doors of the mansion.

"Where are you going?!" he yelled from behind us.

"The Single Girl Rules!" I yelled back to him.

"What the hell are you talking about?!"

I'd always thought Justin was so cool. How did he not know about the Single Girl Rules? #Lame. "I'll be back before the ceremony!"

"Don't you runaway-bride me, missy!"

"I'm not!"

"Don't you dare get in that helicopter!" he screamed

Too late. Luckily the helicopter was already here, ready to whisk me and shmoopie poo away to our honeymoon. We climbed in. "Go, go, go!"

The pilot turned around. "Um. Where?"

He was probably expecting me to yell 'any-where.' But despite what everyone thought, I wasn't a runaway bride. I was so excited to marry my shmoopie poo. But I just needed to do this one thing first.

***

Everyone on campus stared at me as we made our way to the library. Or maybe they were staring at Ash's hideous dress. I smiled to myself.

"Justin has called me 17 times," said Ash. "Just since we landed! We need to get back to the helicopter ASAP."

"Not until the Single Girl Rules are back in their rightful place."

"The ceremony starts in an hour!"

"I know. And this is great practice for my walk down the aisle." I smiled and waved at some rando as I did my graceful walk. I'd practiced it a thousand times.

"Um…so…are we going to go back?"

"We're here!" I ran up the library steps.

"That wasn't an answer to my question!" Ash said as she hurried after me in her hooker heels.

And I don't mean that in a bad way. I think hookers are awesome and I totally respect their lifestyle. I'd met plenty of guys who'd thought I was a hooker. And I always took it as a compliment.

"Why are we at the library?" asked Ash.

"Shhh. Students are studying."

"No, they're all looking at you."

"Huh." I held my head up even higher. Now that I thought about it, any guy here would totally bang me in this dress. Because not only did I look hot AF, but who didn't want to be someone's last shag before they got hitched? But alas...none of these guys looked hot enough. "This way." I grabbed Ash's hand and pulled her up the stairs.

"Seriously, Chastity. We have to get back. Stop messing around. I'm starting to stress sweat and this taffeta shows *everything*."

"I know, it's amazing."

"I hate you."

"No, you love me. And I'm not messing around." I passed one aisle of books and then the next. Which aisle was it? I didn't love the library. I'd rather reread Twilight than pick up some useless textbook. But this had always been a great place to fuck cute college boys. Speaking of which...the guy in the military history aisle was totally eye-fucking me. And I could just tell he had a big cock. Probably at least 8 inches. Maybe more.

"Don't do whatever you're thinking about doing," said Ash.

"What am I thinking about doing?"

"Fucking that guy."

"Wrong! It would be too complicated in this dress to fuck him. I was thinking about blowing him."

"There's no time for that!"

"But I'll be so quick about it. I can totes make him cum in like 2 minutes flat. #NoGagReflex."

Ash stared at me.

"Don't look at me like that. I'm not being bad!"

"Yes you are! It's the day of your wedding and you're thinking about blowing some rando."

"Exactly. It's the *day* of my wedding. As in…my wedding hasn't happened yet. As in, I'm still a single girl. And thus the Single Girl Rules still apply to me."

"Can we please just find this shelf and then get back to the wedding? You know what being late does to me!"

Hmmm… She had a point. She got so weird when she was going to be late. It was one of her greatest fears. And as much as I wanted to torture her for what she'd made me wear at her first wedding, I wasn't *that* cruel. And anyway…I was about to get all the cock I needed on my honeymoon.

I scanned the aisles. Seriously…what the hell had they done when they remodeled this place? Did these basic bitches know nothing about the Dewey

Decimal System? *Ah! There it is*! I yanked Ash into the Russian literature section.

"What the actual fuck is happening right now?" she asked.

I stopped at the third shelf and scanned the spines for... "I got it!" I pulled out the book with the gold edges and maroon cover. I couldn't read a single word in Russian. But one day I'd wandered down this abandoned aisle to make out with some jock. We'd knocked this book off the shelf during our hot make-out sesh. And there the Single Girl Rules were in all their glory. "This is where I found them." I held up the book.

"Right. The whole you-found-them-while-making-out-with-some-hot-jock story. I remember."

"Then why don't you believe me?"

"Because you made the Single Girl Rules up!"

"I did not." I'd never shown the original document to Ash. It was too precious to show to anyone, even to my bestie. But now that I was putting them back, it was time for her to see the rules in all their glory. I lifted up my skirt.

"Stop it! You're going to get us arrested for real this time."

"I'm not stripping. Why do you always shame strippers, anyway? Single Girl Rule #10..."

"I know. Rule #10: All celebrations of important life events must involve strippers. I freaking hate that rule."

"You're not going to like a few things at the wedding then." I lifted my skirt higher and pulled the folded-up piece of paper out of my garter. I'd been putting it there for years. It's where I held all my most sacred belongings. So...the Single Girl Rules and spare condoms. You never knew when you'd need an extra condom. Well, I kind of did. The answer was quite a bit. I was a big believer in one orgasm not being nearly enough. Our bodies were designed to have more than that. #OrgasmFacts.

I unfolded the paper and showed it to Ash.

"What the hell is that? Is that in Russian?"

"Yup. The original Single Girl Rules were in Russian. It took a Russian exchange student a couple of days to translate them."

"That's why you kept hanging out with Slavanka?"

"Yeah. She was super cool."

"I thought you were trying to find a new best friend."

"What? Never. You're my best friend, Ash. Always and forever." I folded the original Single Girl Rules Russian edition back up and tucked it into the book. "I should probably leave the translated version with it, right? That'll make things easier for the next single girl who finds them." I pulled my Single Girl Rules membership card out of my bra and put it in the book too.

"I can't believe they're actually real." Ash looked...*shook*.

"I told you. They're a sacred tradition for single girls all over the world. It's an international thing."

"But...how? All the rules are so...ridiculous."

"They're not ridiculous at all! I mean just look at Rule #1: Boys are replaceable. Friends are Forever."

"Right. That one is normal. That's pretty much the only normal one. And you even make that rule dirty."

She laughed. "I know. Do you remember that night when I first told you about the rules?" It was right after I'd gotten them translated. And I couldn't wait to put them into action.

"Chastity, your wedding starts in..." she looked at her phone. "40 minutes! We need to get back."

"Oh, I think we have some time to reminisce. We need to say goodbye to the Single Girl Rules in style." I did jazz hands and gave Ash a little shimmy for effect.

"Right, by getting your ass married."

"Nope. A montage. We need a montage!" I clapped my hands together.

"You're a crazy person."

"No. I'm a single girl. For another…38 minutes. Que the flashback scenes!"

Ash laughed. "You're going to go through all the rules, aren't you?"

"Is there any other way? It all started on a dark and stormy night…"

"As fun as that sounds, you're going to miss your wedding, Chastity. Maybe you can reminisce on the helicopter."

"Shmoopie poo is amazing in every single way. That includes being a very patient man. He'd wait like ten lifetimes for me. And these flashbacks are important. They all led me to him. It's basically the story of us. And of you and me! And of single girls all over the world!"

"Okay fine. But make it quick."

"Yay montage time! Let's do this damn thing! Where was I?" I cleared my throat. "It all started on a dark and stormy night… Wait! We have to go back even further. Because now that you believe the Single Girl Rules are real, you need to hear exactly how I found them."

"Chastity! You know I hate being late! I'm going to ruin this dress with gallons of sweat."

"On any other day I would love to make you run around fully nude, but not on my wedding day. I'm the star today! Now pop a squat and listen up. It actually all started on a bright and sunny morning…"

Chapter 1

A SHAG IN THE LIBRARY
13 Years Ago - Wednesday - Sept 4, 2013

"Today's going to be a great day!" I said as I pulled on my tightest mini-skirt. I twirled in front of the mirror and turned to my new roommate, Ash. "I can't wait for classes to end so we can go out tonight."

"But it's Wednesday."

"Yeah it is! Hump day!" I froze when my eyes registered her outfit. "What in the actual F are you wearing right now?"

Ash looked down at her t-shirt that was two sizes too big and her baggy sweats. "My first class doesn't start for another three hours."

"So you'll change before that?"

"Yes?"

I put my hand on my hip. "That did not sound very convincing. Girl, you need to show some more skin if you want to find yourself a good bang for this weekend. Try this." I tossed her my second favorite mini-skirt.

She caught it but did not look very excited. "I'm here to study marketing, not bang randos all weekend."

I laughed. "All weekend? I like your style."

"I said I *wasn't* going to bang guys all weekend."

Poor, sweet Ash. I was about to change her whole world. "Get dressed. We're going to find ourselves some men in our classes today."

"Umm...change?" She held the skirt in front of her like a shield. "What about your bodyguards?"

"Oh, them?" I gestured to the two burly men standing in the corner of our room staring at us. "Just pretend they're invisible."

"How do you expect me to pretend that?" Ash hissed.

Hmm. She had a good point. I was used to Ghost and Teddybear following me around. But they'd been especially annoying ever since I came to college. I'd have to figure out a way to ditch them. In the meantime...they were invisible. I pulled off my shirt and changed into a crop top.

Ash just stared at me like I was insane.

"You're so silly, bestie."

She smiled.

I wasn't sure what was going on with her. Was it a body image thing? Because I couldn't find a single thing wrong with changing in front of my two hot bodyguards. Having eyes on my body made me feel fierce. It seemed to make Ash feel the exact opposite. But I got along with her really well. Surprisingly enough, a lot of girls hated me. No idea why.

But I liked Ash. We'd only been living together for a week and we already had dinner together every night. She was my new bestie. And besties helped besties with their self-image. I'd help her break out of her shell in no time. "It's fine. I'll go and take Ghost and Teddybear with me. And then you can change into that." I pointed to the skirt I'd tossed at her. "And this!" I pulled a tank top out of my closet and gave it to her before walking to the door. "See you for dinner?"

"Yeah, that would be great."

"And you better be wearing that! Later!" I left the room and my bodyguards followed me. Yeah, they were definitely getting annoying. Back in high school it was one thing. All my friends understood that Daddy was a little overprotective. But here in college, they were definitely cramping my style. I'd have to call Daddy and fix this. Or ditch them. I'd figure it out. I didn't want them to make me lose my first female friend in ages. Ash came before hot bodyguards 100%. I eyed them over my shoulder. *How do I make you two disappear?*

When I was staring at them over my shoulder I bumped into someone. Literally. No, not just someone. A very handsome someone. Two strong arms caught me. I looked up into dark brown eyes. And the cutest dimple in his left cheek. And that smile? *Yum.*

"Are you alright?" he asked.

"I am now."

He laughed and made sure I was stable before releasing me from his grip. He was taller than I first thought. And his shoulders were so much broader. I bet he could carry me over his shoulder and have his way with me so easily. I bit my lip.

"You new on campus?" he asked. "I haven't seen you around."

"Brand new."

"A freshman?" He raised his eyebrows.

"A freshman with the attitude of a senior who doesn't give a shit."

He laughed.

I looked over my shoulder at my bodyguards. "Speaking of not giving a shit...I have an idea."

"What kind of idea?"

"My first class today is English. Which I speak fluently. So there's no reason for me to go and I really want to ditch."

"And what did you want to do for the next hour instead?" he asked.

"Oh, I don't know." I placed my hand on his chest. "I was thinking...*you*." I watched as his Adam's apple rose and then fell. "But we have to make a run for it."

"What?"

"Come with me." I grabbed his hand and ran off the brick path, pulling him into the grass.

"Where are we going?" he said with a laugh.

"Not here."

"Get back here!" yelled Teddybear.

It just made me run faster. Where could we hide? I looked back and forth over the green. It was tempting to bring him back to my dorm. But for some stupid reason my security guards had access to that. *Damn it, Daddy.* So instead, I ran up the steps of the library hand-in-hand with the broad-shouldered stranger.

He wasn't out of breath at all. He must have been a jock. But he certainly wasn't the first jock I'd hooked up with on campus. So I immediately nick-named him Jock #3 in my head as we ran through the library and up a flight of stairs.

"Shhh!" some evil librarian said to us as we laughed.

Someone needed a big dose of the D.

Jock #3 laughed as I pulled him into the stacks.

We were both out of breath now. But before I had a chance to debate whether or not he was actu-ally a jock or not, he kissed me.

Yes, please.

I grabbed the front of his shirt and pulled him closer to me. Making out with a stranger was so much better than listening to a boring professor drone on and on about a subject I knew all about.

His hands fell to my waist.

I didn't want to waste my precious bodyguard-free time. I figured I had 10 minutes tops until they found me. So I jumped, wrapping my legs around Jock #3's waist.

He wasn't expecting it, and my back slammed against the shelf of books as he steadied himself.

God, this is so fucking hot. We were about to bring the whole library down. I had no idea why, but there was nothing I loved more than making out with a complete stranger. No strings attached fun was a way of life.

His fingers wandered to my ass and he groaned into my mouth.

That was my favorite part. A subtle, uncontrollable groan. *Fuck me please.*

"You're a miracle," he said.

"Yes. But my name's Chastity." That was one of my rules. No banging until they knew my name. I loved being unforgettable. And it was much harder to forget me when men were screaming my name.

"You seem anything but chaste."

How many times had I heard that before? But I didn't care about what came out of his mouth. I just cared about what his mouth could do. "Tell me about it." I grabbed both sides of his face and pulled his lips back to mine. He pushed my back against the shelf of books again and I heard something fall to the floor.

I opened my eyes to see what had fallen. There was a book on the ground, which wasn't surprising. What was surprising was the folded-up note that had fallen out. "Time out," I said and tapped his shoulder.

"Huh?"

Okay, so maybe Jock #3 wasn't a jock at all if he didn't know what a time out was. I wriggled out of his grip and lifted up the note from the book. I unfolded it and stared down at the...list? I wasn't exactly sure what it was because it was not in the English language I was so stellar at. "What language is this?" I lifted up the book too and it was in the same gibberish. But the gold edges made it seem so regal. I was obsessed. Who snuck a secret note into a beautiful book like this? It must be important.

And I had no idea why, but my hand felt all warm and fuzzy holding it. Like I was meant to find this while making out with a complete stranger. Fate. I swore I heard angelic music playing somewhere in the library. Yeah, this was definitely fate.

"I don't know. We're in the Russian lit section. So it's probably that. Let me see it…"

I pulled it to my chest. *No.* Finders keepers. I didn't want his dirty paws on my top-secret note.

"Okay then. How about we get back to what we were doing…"

I patted his arm. Did he not understand the importance of a secret note in a secret book? With gold edging? That made my hand feel warm? That was total fate? Was he dense or something? He certainly wasn't someone I wanted to hook up with in the stacks. So basic. "I have a boyfriend."

"What?"

"Yup. Later." I stared at the note. I felt him staring at me for a beat until he wandered off. It wasn't a lie. I did have a boyfriend. But he was going to a different school, so nothing I did here counted as cheating. That's how life worked. My eyes wandered over the foreign script. The only thing I recognized were a few drawn hearts in the corner. Was it something about love? I honestly didn't know the first thing about love. Maybe it was a list on how to find your true love? I almost laughed out loud. What a ridiculous thought. True love wasn't a thing. Daddy told me so.

"There you are," said Teddybear. "You have to stop running off."

Ghost just stared at me. He never talked, but his stern gaze said it all.

I ignored them. I needed to find a Russian translator ASAP. And I had the perfect person in mind. There was an exchange student in my English class that actually needed English lessons. She'd probably be able to help. I stuffed the note in my backpack. "Time for class, right?"

"Yes."

"Well...that's where I was going, creeper."

"I'm not creeping on you." Teddybear scowled. "Your father is paying me to protect you. And to make sure you go to class."

Nope. He was a hired creeper. I was surprised he wasn't wearing a fake mustache and a trench coat. Such a pediatrist. Or was it a pedophile? He was probably both. And it didn't matter how cute he was. Dirty creepers had to learn their lesson. Besides, he was freaking out my new friend. And I couldn't have that. I'd need to think of something and fast. But right now I just wanted to know what this paper said.

"What did you just put in your backpack?" he asked. "Don't you have to check books out at the front?"

"As if. I'm not a nerd." Not that there was anything wrong with nerds. I loved a man in glasses. Sometimes the geekier the guy, the freakier they were in the sheets. And speaking of geeks...I needed to find that Russian exchange student. I needed to know what this list said.

Teddybear just shrugged.

I blatantly adjusted my girls in front of him, making sure they were pouring out of my top. "Carry me to class? My feet hurt."

"Chastity…"

"Please?" If I was going to have a pediatrist on campus lurking in corners, it might as well be one who carried me around like a princess.

"Why don't you just take off your high heels?"

"And get foot fungus?" Ash had told me all about it. Apparently fungus was everywhere. Thank goodness she'd warned me. "I'd rather die."

He laughed. "Fine. Whatever." He lifted me into his very strong arms.

Yummy. Yeah, getting rid of my security detail would be easy. I already had Teddybear eating out of the palm of my hand. Hopefully figuring out this translation issue would be just as easy. Because I needed to figure out what it said as badly as I needed to get laid tonight. Both were of equal importance. I should really call my boyfriend…

Chapter 2

TITS LOVE MEAT
Wednesday - Sept 4, 2013

"No. Translate it."

"It is paper," Slavanka said.

Slavanka, you whore. She just wasn't getting it. I'd been standing here after class for hours. Or at least, that's how it felt. I was pretty sure it had only been like two minutes, but I was not a woman of much patience. "Translate what is on the paper."

"Paper."

Holy hell. I pulled out a chair and sat down next to her. "See these?" I pointed to the Russian letters. "What does it say?"

"Oh. I see."

"Yeah?"

"Yes, yes." She leaned over to get a better look. "Paper says…Single Girl Rules."

"Oh my God, what?!"

She smiled. "Yes, rules of the single girls."

No freaking way! I needed this in my life ASAP. "That's amazing! What is the first rule?"

"My English is not so good."

"That's okay, just give me the best translation you have."

She looked back down at the paper and tilted her head to the side. "Okay. I will do this. Rule #1 is…Boys are replaceable. Friends are forever."

"That is so true." I was finally learning that very thing. Having Ash as a friend was one of my favorite parts of my college experience so far. Well, that and all the dirty sex. "That's a good solid rule."

"Yes, yes."

"How many rules are there?"

"Very many."

"That makes sense." I'd always had a hard time keeping friends. I probably didn't know some of these rules. "What about this one?" I pointed to a random line on the paper.

"Oh. Oh my. Lots of sex talk."

"Ah!" So it wasn't just about friendship. It was about my favorite subject. *I wonder if it covers anal too…* "I'm so excited!"

She laughed.

"Slavanka, I love you. How long will it take to translate all of these?"

"One day. Two maybe."

"Thank you!" I gave her a big hug. "I don't know how I'll ever repay you. You're seriously the best." I suddenly felt bad for silently calling her a whore a few minutes ago. She wasn't a whore at all. Well…unless she was. Which was fine. I was cool with that. I could tell we were going to be good friends too. Slavanka was a kinky bitch.

***

"You won't even believe what I found today," I said as I bit into another big juicy burger. Another thing I'd learned from Ash…I didn't have to eat salads all the time like my stupid fake friends back in New York. Ash looked amazing and she ate whatever she wanted. And burgers and fries were freaking great. If I was lucky, any weight I did gain would go right to my tits. My tits loved meats and bread.

"What did you find? I just found out that you can take these weird gym glasses that actually count toward credits to your GPA."

"Yeah…what I found out was nothing like that. But now I'm curious. What kind of weird gym classes are we talking about? I've been dying to take pole classes."

"Like pole vaulting?"

I laughed. "No, more of the stripper variety."

"Oh." Ash's eyes grew round. "No, these classes are like…frisbee. Which sucks because I'm terrible at frisbee. Every time I throw one I lose it."

"Like…you throw it too high?"

"No. It like goes over a fence of an evil neighbor never to be seen again. Or on the roof. Or in a tree. That kind of thing."

"We should probably skip taking that class then. Next semester we're totally signing up for everything together."

"We are?"

"Of course. That's what best friends do. And speaking of best friends…that's what I wanted to talk to you about. I was making out with Jock #3 in the library today and a magical book fell from a shelf. And inside was this list of rules to live by. Angelic music started playing in the library. I swear it was like I was in a movie. It was all very mysterious and amazing. And I'm pretty sure we're going to have the best college experience ever. Slavanka's going to translate the rules for me."

"I have no idea what half of what you said means. And who's Slavanka?"

"This super cool Russian exchange student. You'll love her."

"Wait, and she needs to translate the angelic rules?"

"Oh right. I forgot to say. They're in Russian."

"Well of course."

"Right. Fancy rules are never in English. I really need to drop that class."

Ash started laughing. And then she started laughing even harder. "What the hell are you talking about right now? Your train of thought is insane."

"My train of thought? You just talked about taking a frisbee class even though you're a frisbee disappearing act."

She started laughing harder.

Which made me laugh too. I swore, if I'd said something like that to any other girl they would have flipped their hair over their shoulder and walked away. But not Ash. She didn't mind when I told it to her straight. And I was glad she did the same with me.

I tried to stop laughing but it was hard because when Ash laughed her face got all red and for some reason that made me laugh more. "Girl, stop it! Don't you want to know what the first rule is?"

"I thought Slavanka was translating them?"

"Yeah. I'll have the whole list soon. But the first rule is: Boys are replaceable. Friends are forever. I'm going to start living by that motto hard."

"How hard?"

"So. Hard."

"That's what she said!"

I laughed. We'd been binge-watching *The Office* at night before bed. And one of our favorite things was "that's what she said" jokes. I should have seen the hard comment ending that way. I'd totally set her up.

I leaned forward and lowered my voice. "Guess what else is on the list?"

"I don't know. Like other basic girl code stuff probably. Like don't go to the bathroom alone kind of thing."

"These are not basic girl code rules."

"The first one seemed normal enough…"

"Yeah, but the rest of them are filled with sex rules."

"Wait. What?"

"Yeah. Slavanka looked all shocked by the illicit content in the rules. And I am here for it. I've been dying to try anal for a while and I'm so excited to see what the rules say about that."

"Anal? Like…probing?"

"Yes. I think the first time is kinda painful because you have to get a little stretched out first. We should probably do it together."

"No thanks."

"Ash, you have to live a little."

"I like my butthole intact, thank you very much."

I started laughing really hard this time. Which just made her start laughing again.

"Oh my gosh, Ash. I almost forgot to tell you because I was so excited about the Single Girl Rules. We're invited to a party on Friday night."

"Did Jock #3 ask you?"

"No, Jock #3 was a total loser. And his jock status was very questionable. I actually bumped into Jock #1 when I was running late for my second class. Since I'd stayed late to talk to Slavanka and everything."

"Of course. And Jock #1 invited you to the party?"

"Mhm."

"Well there you go. I'm not invited. He invited *you*. I was thinking on Friday I'll just snuggle up in bed and watch more of *The Office*."

"Without me?"

Ash shrugged.

"No way, you slut."

Ash laughed. "Parties aren't really my thing."

"Yeah, but this party is everyone's thing. Rumor has it that the dean has been dying to shut it down for years. It's the first epic party of the school year. And it moves every year to a new location so the dean can't find it. I won't even know where it is until I get the text Friday night. It's all very hush-hush and so freaking cool."

Ash twisted her mouth to the side. It looked like she was maybe considering it.

I knew how to push her over the edge. "And you can't make me go alone or I'll cry."

Now Ash was starting to look very guilty. Which meant I almost had her.

"I could just ask Slavanka…"

"You barely even know Slavanka. What if she's dangerous?"

"Because she's Russian? That's very uncultured of you, Ash. She doesn't seem like a dirty communist."

"No. Like…stranger danger."

"Hmmm. That is a good point. If only I had someone to go with me…"

Ash sighed.

"Plus everyone's going to be talking about this party for months. It's the party to end all parties. The rager to end all ragers. The epicness to end all epicness."

"Promise you won't ditch me?"

"I would never."

Ash just stared at me. "Do you not remember our first night here when you dragged me out to that frat house on Main Street and disappeared?"

"Like one of your frisbees?"

"Stop it. I turned around and you were gone. Actually, if I recall correctly it was because you were hooking up with Jock #1. So the fact that he's the one who invited you to this party is making me even more nervous. I had to walk home alone past midnight. It was very scary."

"If I recall correctly, one of my bodyguards went with you."

"Yeah, but those guys creep me out. You know this."

We both turned toward my bodyguards who were standing in the corner of the dining hall staring at us.

I'd take care of them soon. There had to be a way to get rid of them. I just hadn't figured it out yet. "I'm sorry," I said. "I won't ditch you again. I promise." I lifted my hand up. "Pinky promise."

Ash reluctantly wrapped her pinky around mine. "Pinky promise."

"Unless there's a really hot guy…"

"Chastity!"

I laughed and let go of her pinky. "There's nothing to worry about. On Friday night I'm gonna try to find us some guys that are down for the back door."

"No."

"Yes!"

"No!"

"Is everything okay here?" asked Teddybear. Ghost glared at us.

"Yes," I said. "We were both just talking about how we've never had anal and are dying to try. Have you tried it?" I winked at him.

He cleared his throat. "So you're both okay?"

"Well, not until we do the dirty deed. And I'd much prefer to do it with someone I know and trust. Someone really...strong." My eyed landed on the big biceps hidden beneath his suit jacket. "If you know what I'm saying."

He didn't respond.

"Well endowed is what I'm saying."

He cleared his throat again. "If you need anything, I'll be over there." He walked away.

I turned back to Ash and sighed. "How simple is he? I just told him I needed anal. Clearly I do need something and he just walked away. It was a very open invitation. He's not very good at serving me."

"Isn't he just supposed to protect you? Not serve you sexually? And maybe he's not into that kinky stuff."

"I wasn't going to dress him up in leather or whip him or anything."

"Fair."

I laughed. "Ash, you are seriously the best. So you're coming to the party, right? Please? Pretty, pretty please?"

"I guess I have no choice."

"Exactly." I lifted up a fry and bit into it. *Holy greasy goodness.* I couldn't wait to see if my tits grew before Friday night. Because I needed to look fine as hell. I wanted to make sure that all the boys at this school knew I had arrived.

Chapter 3
SEXY TWINS GAMBIT
Friday - Sept 6, 2013

My phone buzzed and Slavanka's name crossed the screen. I almost screamed as I answered it. "Tell me they're ready."

"The rules are ready," Slavanka said.

"Ah I love you!"

"Yes, okay."

"Can I come get them now?"

"It is rain weather. You come tomorrow."

I looked out the window of my dorm. A rainy day had turned into a dark and stormy night. But rain had never stopped me from going to a party before. Besides, Jock #1 was the best of the jocks I'd hooked up with since coming to campus. To-night was going to be a blast. Especially if I had the Single Girl Rules in my hands. "I'll come now."

"If you are sure."

"Mhm. See you soon." I ended the call and turned to Ash. "They're ready."

"What's ready?"

I'd been talking about nothing but the Single Girl Rules since they'd magically appeared to me two days ago. How did she not know what I was talking about right now? "The Single Girl Rules."

"Oh, right. The paper that fell from the sky with angelic music playing that's full of sex rules?"

"It fell from a book, but yes. I'm going to go grab them. Want to come?"

"No, I need to figure out what to wear tonight. What do you think of this?" She pulled out what I assumed was something she'd stolen from her grandmother for a reason I couldn't fathom. It. Was. Horrifying.

"Um…keep looking," I said. "I'll be back soon."

"Wait, hasn't the party already started? We're going to be late."

"Of course we're going to be late. You can't show up to a party on time. That would be #Lame."

"Oh. Right. I knew that." Ash scrunched her mouth to the side and looked at Ghost and Teddy-bear in the corner.

I laughed. "Don't worry, I'm taking them with me. See you in a bit. And try to find something with a little less…sleeves."

"It doesn't have sleeves."

I tilted my head to the side. How did it not have sleeves? There was so much fabric. Where was it all going? "If you say so. It's still a no from me."

Ash nodded and shoved the hideous dress back into her closet. I'd definitely need to dress her when I got back. Which was fine. I was already planning to. I left the room with my two minions in toe.

"When are you going to tell Ash that you aren't allowed to go to the party?" asked Teddybear.

I laughed and shoved his arm. "Oh Teddybear. You're so funny. I talked with Daddy earlier today and he said it was fine."

"You know I'm going to text him to confirm that, right?"

Damn it! "Fine. I know I'm not allowed to go." *Because of you, you jerk.* I still couldn't believe he'd ratted me out to my dad and gotten me banned from any more parties just because I kept ditching their lame asses. It wasn't my fault that they couldn't keep up with me. "I'm just pretending like I can for Ash's benefit. That poor girl really needs to break out of her shell. I'm gonna get her all ready and then break the news to her at the last minute. By that point she will have spent so much time getting ready that it won't make sense for her to back out."

"That's very thoughtful of you."

I nodded. But my mind was elsewhere. I was running out of time to come up with a plan to ditch these idiots. There was no way I was going to miss the party of the century.

A few days ago I would have just been able to run away from them. But they'd gotten wise to my tricks and swapped their dress shoes out for running shoes. It was dreadfully annoying to not be able to ditch them, but I had to admit that the combination of suits and running shoes did something to my lady bits.

When we got to the exit, I stopped. "Umbrella me."

Ghost just stared at me like I was insane.

Gah. "Not you, little grumpkin." I stepped around him to look at Teddybear. "Umbrella me."

Like a good little boy, he opened up my umbrella for me just as I stepped out into the rain. Not a drop of rain fell on me. But he got absolutely drenched.

What? It wasn't my fault he didn't bring an umbrella for himself. Besides, I was teaching them both a lesson. The lesson was a simple one. I didn't want them here. They were terrifying my new bestie and I couldn't have that. So if they stuck around I was going to make them miserable.

It didn't take us long to reach Slavanka's dorm. She opened up the door for us and her eyes landed on my dripping wet security detail. Her eyes grew round.

Yeah, I got it. I had two very delicious body-guards. But they were also the worst. If they followed her around, she'd understand.

"Ignore them," I said. "Do you have the rules?"

She lifted up the original document and I swore I heard harps playing. If I'd been facing the windows, I bet the rain would have stopped and a rainbow would have appeared for the two seconds before she handed me the Russian original and the English translation.

I exhaled slowly. It felt like I was holding the most important document ever written. Like more important than the Declaration of Independence. Who cared about some dumb complaints written by a bunch of old dudes? These rules had been written by a sexy Russian goddess, I just knew it. And I was #TeamGoddess. "Wow they feel...heavy."

"It is paper."

Those were the first words she'd ever said to me. We'd gone full circle. "Slavanka you funny bitch." I looked down at the list. I didn't have time to read all the rules right now. Technically the party had already started. And I didn't want to be more than two hours late. Two hours late was exactly the right vibe I wanted to present to Jock #1. Not desperate, but also the classic "I bothered to show up so fuck me" attitude. And I needed every minute of time remaining to wrassle Ash into a suitable slutty number.

But one rule caught my eye. The perfect rule. Rule #19: Never wear the same dress as a friend, unless you're attempting the sexy twins gambit.

OMG. O. M. Freaking. G! I looked over at my bodyguards. I still didn't know how to get rid of them for good, those drenched bastards. But I 100% knew how to go to the party and ditch them for longer than I ever had before. The Single Girl Rules were an amazing blessing. And I needed to make sure I didn't get them as wet as my body-guards were. So I did the only reasonable thing I could think of. I folded the rules up and slipped them into my bra. They'd be safe in there from the rain.

"Thanks, Slavanka," I said. "See you in class!"

"Yes."

I waved goodbye and hurried back to my dorm. But when I reached my building I stopped. "You can't come up while we're changing."

Ghost lowered his eyebrows at me.

"You two perverts are freaking out Ash. So you stay here like the good boys you are. I'll be down in thirty minutes. Ish."

"Down for what?" Teddybear asked. "I texted your father, and you are absolutely *not* allowed out tonight. Or any night until your father deems it safe."

"That's a shame. I guess you'll just be standing out here all night then."

"We're not going to stand out here in the rain."

"Why? Because you want to creep on me and Ash changing for the party? I wonder what Daddy would think about that…"

"We'll stand guard in the hallway, then."

Damn. That would make my plan more difficult. But not impossible.

They escorted me up to my room. I blew them a kiss as the door thudded behind me. I was surprised that Ash wasn't in the room. Hopefully she was putting on tons of makeup in the bathroom, although I found that pretty unlikely.

I quickly changed into the outfit I'd picked out earlier. And since Ash still wasn't back, I pulled out the Single Girl Rules and started reading them. The first section was labeled "10 commandments":

1. Boys are replaceable. Friends are forever.
2. Girls' night is every Friday. No exceptions.
3. Never let a friend go into a bathroom alone.
4. You can never have too many shoes.
5. Have wine in your purse at all times.
6. Always kiss and tell.
7. Pics or it didn't happen.

8. If a man has 8 abs and 8 inches, he may not be refused.

9. If you hear about a well-hung man, share the news.

10. All celebrations of important life events must involve strippers.

Dear lord. These are perfect! They were exactly what I'd been missing in my life. I couldn't believe how many of them I'd been violating. Like not having a girls' night every Friday. And what the heck had I been doing not taking pictures of all my lovers?

Speaking of which…

Oh my God! That's it! It was suddenly so clear to me how I was going to solve my bodyguard issue once and for all. I was frankly ashamed that I hadn't figured out this solution earlier. I could already see a classic seduction blackmail plan forming in my head. It was an oldie but a goodie and it had been right in front of me the whole freaking time. For the first time ever, I felt a little basic. I shook the thought away. It wouldn't do any good to dwell on that, though, because obvs I wasn't actually basic. But more importantly…there were more Single Girl Rules to read!

One read-through was all it took to commit these bad boys to memory. Most material took me two passes, but these just made sense. It didn't feel like I was learning, it was more like I was reading an innate truth about the very essence of life.

The door of our dorm creaked open. I placed the rules down on my bed. I didn't want to take them with me to the party because with my new plan there was a 100% chance I was going to end up naked. The rules wouldn't be safe in my bra tonight.

"Jesus, Chastity," said Ash, covering her eyes. "What are you wearing?"

"Uh, a super cute outfit?" I twirled my leather leash around but froze when I saw what outfit she'd landed on. "The real question is, what are *you* wearing? I hate to do this, but I'm going to have to invoke Single Girl Rule #17: Friends don't let friends wear ugly outfits. #RealTalk." I freaking loved these rules.

Ash looked down at her frumpy t-shirt with the saddest look on her face. It was soul-crushing. I never wanted to see her that sad again.

"Just kidding. You look hot." I reached out and gave her boobs two very complimentary honks.

Her sadness morphed into utter bewilderment. "Did you just grab my boobs?"

"Uh, yeah. Single Girl Rule #20: You may squeeze your friend's boob no more than twice to compliment a good outfit."

"Wait, are those really in the rules?"

"Mhm. I'll show you later."

"Aren't they right there?" She looked over at my bed, but I stepped in front of her.

"There's no time for this!" Ash looked like a homeless person. This was an emergency situation. "I'll recite them for you later. And I do love your outfit." I tried not to gag at the lie. "But...tonight you have to dress in something I'd wear."

"Why?"

"Because I have a master plan." I threw a sexy little black number at her and then dug a blonde wig out of my closet. I was always prepared for any wardrobe emergency. "Put that on."

"Why do you have a wig that looks like your hair?"

"Just in case I go all Britney and shave it off. You never know what a drunken night can lead to. Everyone in the spotlight is bound to have a moment. Now put it on and let's get going."

"Why exactly am I dressing like you?"

"Because I have a way to get rid of Ghost and Teddybear." That got her attention. "For the life of me I couldn't figure out how to ditch them. But then I saw Rule #19: Never wear the same dress as a friend, unless you're attempting the sexy twins gambit. And then I saw Rule #7: Pics or it didn't happen, and everything kinda fell into place. It is so on."

"The sexy twins what?"

"I'll explain more later. First change."

Ash sighed and looked down at the outfit. "This dress looks more like a shirt."

"Thank you."

She shook her head, but instead of protesting anymore, she changed. And she looked almost as good blonde as she did with red hair.

"Is my butt hanging out?" Ash asked.

"Only a little."

She looked down her back. "How will this get rid of your bodyguards exactly? Is my ass really gross enough to scare them off?"

"Girl, no. Your ass is beautiful. Here, come closer. It's makeover time."

She stuck her tongue out at me.

But I ignored it. I even applied a perfect layer of lipstick around that tongue. I was pretty talented, thank you very much. After all, I'd been doing my own hair and makeup ever since I was five. Except for special occasions of course. I wasn't a barbarian.

When I was finished with the mascara I stepped back. "You look amazing." My work here was done. "Now get going." I gestured to the door.

"Um…aren't we going to the party together?"

I put my hands on her shoulders and prepared myself for her fury. "No."

"What the hell, Chastity! You promised you wouldn't ditch me and now you're ditching me before we even go!"

"Technically you're ditching me. But just trust me."

"I don't even know where the party is."

"Oh, right. Get this. The dean is hellbent on shutting this party down. So Jock #1's frat set up this whole scavenger hunt that they're going to lead him on all over campus. And the whole time the party is going to be happening at the dean's mansion."

"I'm out." Ash started pulling her dress over her head.

"Whoa, hold on." I put my hand on her arm to stop her from taking her dress off and ruining her hair. "What's wrong?"

"I'm not going to go to a rager at the dean's mansion. We're all going to get arrested and end up in prison. And I'm not built for that. I don't even know how to carve a shank, much less how to keister it."

"Well maybe if you'd try anal with me then you'd be better prepared for such things. Anyway, here's the plan." I leaned in and whispered. "Teddybear said I'm not allowed to go to the party. So you're going to run out of the room dressed like me and make a mad dash for the exit. While those dumb-dumbs chase you, I'll sneak out."

"So I'm just your decoy?" asked Ash. "You don't actually want me at the party?" She sounded so sad.

"What? Of course I want you at the party. As soon as the guards realize that they've been duped they'll leave you alone and try to hunt me down. Which will give you the perfect opportunity to come to the party too. It's the perfect plan."

"Are you sure we shouldn't just stay in and watch *The Office*? I feel like that's so much better than going to prison." She looked longingly at the TV.

"Prison? I don't think so. Single Girl Rule #29: Single girls don't get speeding tickets." I knew it didn't quite apply in this situation, but damn I loved quoting these rules.

"Having an illegal party at the dean's house is a little more serious than a speeding ticket. We could get booked for a million different things. Underage drinking. Breaking and entering. Conspiracy to rape private property. Treason!" She got more frantic with every word.

"So first of all those aren't even all real crimes. And second of all...I'm kind of hoping we do get arrested tonight. Have you seen how hot the campus police officers are? I'll tell you what - if we get arrested, you can have first dibs on which officer you want to fuck."

"No way. Nope. Uh uh." Ash shook her head.

"Suit yourself. If you want me to have all the fun, I'm not going to complain. Anyway, let's get back to the plan. I feel like they're going to catch you pretty quickly, so maybe flirt with them a bit to buy me some extra time. Bonus points if you slap their butts and make fun of their little dicks. I'll see you in a half-hour at the dean's house."

"I'm not going to talk about their penises."

"But it would really help."

"No."

"Yes!"

"Chastity!"

I laughed. "Fine. Just make sure you get around the corner so they don't see me sneak out. Go get 'em, Chastity #2."

"Don't call me that." She exhaled slowly. "I'll see you in half an hour."

"Make sure you keep your head down," I reminded her as I opened the door and shoved her out into the hall.

"Hey!" yelled Teddybear. "Stop!"

As soon as their footsteps faded into the distance, I grabbed my umbrella, opened the door, and slipped out.

Phase 1 was complete. And if I do say so myself, it was executed perfectly. All thanks to the Single Girl Rules telling me about the sexy twins gambit. I hated to think about how much of a basic bitch I was before I found those glorious rules.

If phase 2 went as well, my bodyguards would soon be a distant, sexy memory.

Chapter 4

ROAD HEAD
Friday - Sept 6, 2013

Thunder rumbled and I shivered.

For the first time since coming onto campus, I kind of wish my bodyguards were with me. It was a little creepy to be walking alone at night without protection. But...this was for Ash. Sacrifices had to be made for besties. Single Girl Rule #1: Boys are replaceable. Friends are forever. And I was going to take that very literally. *Goodbye you naughty little stalker boys.*

I made it about half a block before I heard my bodyguards yelling behind me. Or, more accurately, my bodyguard. Singular. Teddybear was screaming bloody murder, but Ghost was as quiet as ever.

Damn it, Ash! How had she only distracted them for like 2 minutes? Had she not even pulled her tits out? I'd have to have a little chat with her about that. But first I had to lose my guards.

Ditching my amazing shoes was not an option. So I did the only rational thing - I ran out into oncoming traffic and put my hand out in the universal "stop" signal.

The driver obeyed, but just barely in time. He laid on his horn as the car skidded to a stop with only a few feet to spare.

"Dude, what the hell?" I said as I shook out my umbrella and climbed into the passenger seat of the car. "You almost hit me."

He stared at me. He might have said something, but I was too distracted by his handsome face. And his forearms. And that cologne. Most guys on campus smelled like cheap beer, but he smelled like fresh grass and sawdust.

"402 West Main Street, please," I said.

"What?"

"402 West Main Street. And step on it. I'm in a hurry." I showed him the map on my phone in case he was deaf or something. We didn't have time to screw around. My bodyguards would be on us in a second.

"Right, I heard you. But this isn't an Uber. You can't just get in and expect me to drive you across campus."

"Of course I can."

"No, you…" He stopped short as I unzipped his pants and pulled his cock out. "What are you…*fuck*," he hissed as I leaned over and took his cock into my mouth.

"Go," I moaned around his length.

He immediately hit the gas.

Good boy.

My hands and lips worked in unison as he kept growing. And growing. And growing. *God damn.* I had hit the jackpot. I tightened my grip and swirled my tongue around his thick shaft. Each groan told me I was closer to getting my reward. Which was good, because we didn't have much time. According to google maps, the dean's mansion was only like a five-minute ride away from my dorm.

Ha. Five minutes. No guy could last five minutes with my mouth on their cock. Unless I wanted them to last. Which in this case…I kind of did. He was bigger than Jock #1, 2, and 3. And he was definitely bigger than my boyfriend. It would feel so good to climb on top of him as soon as we arrived. But no…I couldn't get distracted. I had to stick to the plan.

He hit a speedbump and his cock slid all the way into my throat.

"Oh fuck," he groaned.

So you like my throat, huh? I reached back, grabbed one of his hands, and put it on my head. He immediately pushed my head down again.

I gagged, but only to make him feel good. My gag reflex didn't exist - not since I'd spent a summer in high school deepthroating every banana I could get my hands on. And then I'd graduated to plantains.

I could have made him cum right then and there, but I didn't feel like chatting with him afterwards. So I slowed down a little until it felt like it had been about five minutes. Then I slid my hand down and massaged his balls as I picked up the pace. He grew harder, if that was even possible. And when he pushed on my head to jam his cock all the way down my throat, I knew that it was time for my prize. But since his cock was so far down my throat, I hardly even got to taste his delicious cum. *No fair!* I'd worked hard for that.

I waited until he was all spent and then sat up. My timing was perfect, because we'd just pulled up to the front door of an old brick mansion. Strobe lights poured out of the windows, and I could already feel the bass in the seat of the car.

"Thanks for the ride," I said as I wiped a little cum off my lips. God, what I would do to have a few more minutes so he could bury his face in my pussy. But alas, time was limited. Besides, he'd already given me a ride for my time. I kissed his cheek, grabbed my umbrella, and hopped out.

A line of students wrapped around the side of the mansion. But I wasn't some basic bitch, so I walked right up the stairs. It wasn't like they were going to turn me away…I was barely wearing anything.

I gave the security guy a little wave as I passed. And then a horrible thought occurred to me. I hadn't told my driver my name! *Damn it!* That beautiful man would have thought about Chastity Morgan every time he got into a car for the rest of his life. But he didn't know my name. So now he'd just forever remember me as the perfect 10 who gave him the world's best road head.

Oh well. I could live with that.

In fact…I kind of liked that better. Now that I thought about it, him not knowing my name made it so much more mysterious. When I became famous someday, he'd always see me on TV and wonder - is that the road head goddess?

I walked past the couples grinding and peered into a few corners. I had a feeling that was where I'd find Ash. But I was three corners in and she wasn't anywhere to be found. *Where are you hiding, Ash?*

"There you are!" yelled Jock #1 over the music. "I thought you weren't going to show."

See? Two hours late works every time. "Sorry, I had another thing."

"What?" He cupped his hand to his ear like that would help him hear me over the music blasting.

"Nothing. Let's dance!" I grabbed his hand and dragged him towards the dance floor.

Despite the dean's family room being so spacious, the floor was *packed*. Which was perfect. I loved the energy of tons of people dancing. Nothing beat the feeling of music flowing through me as I grinded up on Jock #1. Well, that wasn't true. Sex was better. But dancing was a close second.

"Dude!" yelled some guy who had just draped his arm around Jock #1's shoulders. "We got in!"

"For real?" said Jock #1.

"Yup. Come check it out."

Jock #1 grabbed my hand and we followed his friend to a pair of rich wooden doors. Inside, six guys in ski masks lounged around the dean's desk. One of them had his feet up on the desk while the rest stood around him. It looked like a scene straight out of a news report about a coup d'etat. The only difference was these guys were wielding wooden frat paddles and golf clubs instead of AK-47s.

"Holy shit," said Jock #1. "We really did it!"

"Yeah we did," said the guy in the chair. He hoisted a red solo cup into the air. "Here's to Alpha Omicron." They all laughed as someone on the other side of the room snapped a photo. And then they took another just to be sure no one blinked.

I had to hand it to them. It was super ballsy to throw this party in the first place. But it was even more ballsy to then take a photo in the dean's office. And as a final cherry on top, they'd spray-painted their frat letters across the dean's portrait. Unless their parents were as rich as Daddy, they were for sure gonna get expelled.

The guy at the desk popped up, took off his mask, and walked over to us. "So, Topher," he said. "This must be the girl you've told us so much about."

Jock #1's name is Topher? Gross.

"Yup," said Topher. "Chastity, meet Cornelius Buttersworth III."

"Call me Trip." He pulled off his Alpha Omicron t-shirt to reveal a perfectly pressed pink polo underneath.

Yeah, definitely a trust fund kid.

They introduced me to the rest of the guys, but I kind of forgot all their names when the last guy pulled off his ski mask. Because he wasn't a stranger. Well, he kind of was. But not completely. Because he was the guy I'd blown on the way here.

Apparently he was good friends with Jock #1.

Oops. But let's be honest - I never would have passed up that cock. It was the perfect ratio of length to girth.

"This is Tenderfoot," said Trip. "If you ever need anything, just ask him for it and he'll fetch it. Isn't that right?"

"Sir, yes sir!" said Tenderfoot.

"I think you and I are going to get along quite well, Tenderfoot," I said with a knowing smile. The poor guy must have been a new pledge or something. But the joke was on the rest of them, because I'd just given him a sweet blowjob. And his cock was way nicer than Jock #1's. Sorry, I mean Topher's. God, I couldn't get over how dumb that name was.

"Shall we get back to dancing?" asked Topher.

"I have a better idea. How about you show me to the master bedroom?" I bit my lip and handed him my leash.

All his frat brothers cheered for him.

"It would be my pleasure," said Topher. He started to lead me out of the room.

At the last second I turned back. "Oh, Tenderfoot? Can you watch the front door for me? If you see a sexy redhead in a tight black dress, send her up to us. Or she might be blonde. Whatever. You'll know when you see her. She's gorgeous but shy, like the cute quirky girl from a romcom." *Was that enough info? Oh!* "Her ass will be hanging out and she'll probably trip up the stairs or something. Thanks!" I blew him a kiss and let Topher pull me upstairs.

If his frat brothers had been excited before, now they were doubly excited. Or perhaps *triply* would be more appropriate, since they thought he was gonna get a threesome.

Ah, how wrong they were…

Chapter 5

SETTING THE TRAP
Friday - Sept 6, 2013

"Are you sure this is the master suite?" I asked. "It feels more like the dean's least favorite child's room."

Topher looked at me like I was crazy. "This is definitely the master suite."

"But there's only one sitting area." I poked my head into the bathroom. "And the bathroom doesn't even have a fireplace." *What kind of mansion is this?* "Oh, I think I get it. This is just some sort of ornamental house. And the dean lives somewhere much nicer. Is that how you guys got away with throwing a party here?"

"The dean definitely lives here. And we got away with this party thanks to the epicness of the one and only Harvey Wallbanger. He's the one who somehow figured out how to lead the dean on a wild goose chase all over town. Dude's a freaking legend."

"Wallbanger, huh?" I leaned back against the tiled bathroom wall, imagining what this Harvey Wallbanger character might do to me if he was here. I bet his epicness extended into the bedroom as well. "Is that his real name, or has he done something to earn that nickname?"

Topher stepped towards me. "If anyone in our frat deserves the nickname Wallbanger, it's me."

"Oh really? Because the first time we banged, you busted in like 2 minutes. We didn't even get past missionary."

Topher waved my comment off. "In my defense, you're extremely hot."

"Fair point. Maybe this time it'll help if we start out with more space between us." I walked over to one of the dean's closets. "Get in."

"What?"

I shoved a few suits aside and pushed him into the closet. Then I closed the door. "I'm going to go get undressed. Holler at me if I go to a spot where you can't see me."

"Okay..." he said. His voice was muffled through the slatted closet door. I didn't blame him for being confused. But I wasn't just being weird - this was all part of my master plan to get rid of my dumb bodyguards once and for all. And I had to make sure this was the perfect room before I initiated phase 2.

I walked over to the loveseat in the farthest corner of the sitting room and started to unzip my dress.

"Hey!" yelled Topher. "I can't see you over there!"

Noted. I went to the couch to give him a better view as I unzipped my dress a little more. "Can you see me now?"

"Yeah!"

I went over and grinded on the bedpost. "How about now?"

"Oh yeah."

I let my dress fall to the ground, leaving me in nothing but lingerie, heels, and my leash. And then a heard a knock at the door. *Finally!* "Come in!" I called as I twirled around the bedpost.

Ash and Tenderfoot walked in. Ash's eyes got big. "Ah! Why are you so naked?!"

I looked down. I would hardly call being in lingerie "so naked." This was more clothing than I usually wore.

She threw her hands over her eyes and ran out of the room. Or…tried to. She misjudged where the door was, so she just ran straight into the wall and flopped backwards on the floor.

Is she dead? "Oh my God, Ash! Are you okay?" I ran over to her.

She kept her eyes firmly shut. "Did I just walk in on you banging someone?"

"Uh, no. Clearly I was just doing a little impromptu pole dance. Come on, open your eyes and get up."

"If I open my eyes, do you promise I'm not going to see something weird? Because my head kinda hurts and I really don't want to accidentally run into the wall again."

"I promise. Wait, does Topher coming out of the closet count as something weird?"

"Topher?" she asked.

"Hot Jock #1." I helped her to her feet.

"Oh. Eh, I guess that wouldn't be that weird. I mean, I haven't met the guy. But from what you've told me, I'm honestly not that shocked to hear that he's batting for the other team."

"Wait," said Tenderfoot. "Topher's a queer?"

"I'm not gay!" yelled Topher as he burst out of the closet. In an unfortunate twist of fate, he'd gotten tangled up with some very colorful silk neckties. That and his lavender polo weren't exactly helping his case.

Ash screamed again and ran for the door. Tenderfoot had closed it though, so she just ran straight into the closed door.

Tenderfoot and I burst out laughing while Topher huffed and puffed and tried to untangle himself from the dean's collection of flamboyant neckties.

Topher glared at Tenderfoot. "Get out of here. And don't ever tell anyone about...this." He finally unwrapped one final tie and tossed it angrily to the ground.

"Sir, yes sir!" yelled Tenderfoot. He bowed and left the room without running into anything.

Topher smoothed his shirt and casually leaned against the wall. "So this is your friend, huh? She's pretty hot."

"Damn right she is. My roomie is the hottest."

Ash looked away.

"You guys ready for some fireworks?" asked Topher.

"Oh my God, yes! I love fireworks. Daddy would always put on the best fireworks show for my birthday when I was little. Although sometimes it scared the ponies..."

"I meant sexual fireworks."

"Oh." I made a pouty face. "But now you got me all excited for real fireworks. What do you think, Ash? Do we need some real fireworks?"

"Sure?" she said. She still seemed a little dazed from her double concussion and was trying to block her view of me with her hands.

"I think we have some sparklers back at the frat house," said Topher.

"Sparklers?" I scoffed. "How insulting. Are you saying that a threesome with us isn't worth the good stuff?"

"Threesome?!" asked Ash. It looked like she was a second away from attempting to run out of the room again.

Topher pulled his shirt off. "How about we do the threesome first, and I'll get some amazing fireworks for another night?"

"Nope." I shook my head. "Fireworks first."

"I don't even know where to buy the good stuff. I'm gonna have to drive all the way to Pennsylvania. Or maybe Maryland would have some?"

I shrugged. "No idea. But you better hurry. It's getting late."

"For real?"

"Yup."

"Damn it. Okay. Wait here and I'll be back soon." He pulled his shirt back on and headed towards the door.

"Wait!" I said. I pulled out my phone and posed next to him for a snap. "I want all my followers to see who throws the most epic parties."

He hid his face. "Whoa, chill. What if the dean sees that?!"

"Uh...you guys just took a picture in his office. And you literally spray-painted your frat letters on his portrait. He's definitely gonna know it was you who threw this party."

Topher laughed. "Those aren't our letters. I'm in Epsilon Pi Beta…not Alpha Omicron."

"Alpha beta what?" I asked.

"The alphas are our rivals. Their president banged Trip's girlfriend. So we're gonna make the dean think they threw this party. If we're lucky, those assholes will get kicked off campus once and for all."

"Oooh." Now the ski masks made sense.

"In that case…" I took a super cute selfie and then added the caption: "This alpha party at the dean's house is EPIC!!!" Then I gave Topher a little slap on the butt. "What are you waiting for? I want my fireworks!"

"Right. I'll be back soon." He looked longingly at my beautiful breasts (this push-up bra was AMAZEBALLS, or else my new meat and bread diet was on point) and then headed out the door.

"You know I'm not going to have a threesome with that douche," said Ash the second he was gone.

"Yeah, I know. I just had to figure out a way to get him out of here for a while so that we can execute Operation Seduction Blackmail. Speaking of which…the bodyguards should be here any minute." I shoved Ash backwards into the closet and slammed it shut. "Start filming and don't come out until I give you the signal. Unless you want to join. Actually, no. Sorry. You can't leave your post. But you can always hop in next time. Don't worry, girl. We're gonna get you that D soon." I checked the mirror to make sure my makeup was on point - spoiler alert: of course it was - and then headed downstairs.

The trap was set.

Chapter 6

SEDUCTION BLACKMAIL
Friday - Sept 6, 2013

While Ash stayed hidden in the closet, I went down and started dancing on tables. All the guys seemed to appreciate my lingerie, but the girls at the party started giving me dirty looks. Which was weird, because I was totally following the Single Girl Rules. Specifically Rule #16: Either your legs, cleavage, or stomach must be showing at all times. Preferably all three.

It made sense that these basic bitches didn't know the rules yet, though. I mean, they'd just been translated. I made a mental note to print up some copies to post around campus. And then I kept dancing my ass off. This DJ was freaking amazing. It was *so* tempting to go blow him, but I didn't want to have my head down behind the DJ booth when Ghost and Teddybear arrived.

After what felt like forever, the two dumb-dumbs finally arrived.

I jumped up and rode a chandelier Miley-Cyrus-in-Wrecking-Ball style to make sure I got their attention. Then I jumped off and ran upstairs.

They ran after me, pushing drunk frat boys out of the way like they were nothing. It was men against boys, and I'm not gonna lie - it was kinda hot.

I dashed into the upstairs bedroom where Ash was creeping in a closet. And then I pretended to fumble with the latch on a window as my bodyguards stormed in.

"That's enough, Chastity," said Teddybear. His voice was so commanding.

I turned around and pretended to be shocked to see him. "Oh, hey. What are you guys doing here? I didn't realize you had gotten an invite." They hadn't, obvs. But they had definitely seen my snap. Everything was going according to plan.

"Don't act like you didn't see us downstairs."

"Oh, you caught my table dance? Did you see the whole thing? Or just the chandelier swing at the end? Because you really need to see the whole thing to understand the narrative of the dance. Want to head back downstairs and I can show you? I may have to flash the DJ to get him to play the song again, but that's fine."

"Time to go back to your dorm," said Teddybear. "It's well past your curfew."

I rolled my eyes. "Why do I even have a stupid curfew?"

"For the same reason you're at the University of New Castle instead of Harvard."

"I have a stupid curfew because the guys at the University of New Castle are rumored to have bigger cocks than the guys at Harvard?" I thought about it for a second and then nodded. "I guess that kinda checks out. But I didn't think Daddy cared about such things."

"What? No. You're here - and have a curfew - because your father is concerned that there are people out there who want to hurt you to hurt him."

"Oh really?" I stepped towards my guards. "And what might those bad men do to me?"

"Kidnap you," said Teddybear.

"That's all? That doesn't sound so bad."

"I assure you, being kidnapped is not a pleasant experience. Which is why you're lucky to have us. And why you need to follow our instructions to stay safe."

"So when you say that they'd kidnap me…what exactly does that entail?"

"For a beautiful girl like you? Nothing good."

I fanned myself. "Aw, Teddybear. You think I'm beautiful?"

"No."

"No I'm not beautiful? Then why were you staring at my tits the other day while I changed?" I did a little shimmy in my lingerie to get my point across.

"I…" He cleared his throat. "Let's go back to the dorm."

"Do you think my kidnapper would stare at my tits while I changed? I think you might need to show me exactly what he'd do. Then maybe I'd have a reason to stop running away from you."

He stared at me.

"Would he like…sell my body to the highest bidder?" I ran my hands down my bare stomach. "Or maybe I'd be his little whore. Any time he wanted, he'd force me to get on my knees and wrap my lips around his thick cock." I slowly put my entire index finger into my mouth and seductively pulled it out.

Both guards stared at me. I had them right where I wanted them.

"Am I getting warmer? Oooh. Maybe they'd take me out on a boat with all their friends and let everyone take turns fucking my tight little pussy." I glanced down at their crotches as I spoke. The growing tents told me everything I needed to know.

I was pretty sure they were seconds away from tossing me on the bed and showing me *exactly* how a kidnapper would treat me.

"It's my job to make sure you never find out," said Teddybear.

Damn it! How was he resisting tearing this lingerie off of me? My seductive powers had never failed me like this before. Then I realized I was going about this all wrong. My bodyguards weren't like the horny frat boys downstairs who would jump any girl with a pulse. My bodyguards were *men*. So I had to seduce them accordingly.

"It's your job to keep me safe, huh? Well that's not very reassuring since you aren't even man enough to show me how scary a kidnapping can be. It's funny…I came to this university because I heard that the guys had big cocks, but so far I've been kinda disappointed. And now I'm learning that my bodyguards don't even have balls."

"That's enough, you mouthy bitch," growled Ghost. "One more word and I'm going to show you exactly how big my balls are."

Holy shit! Ghost talked! That was legit the first time I'd ever heard him speak. "You've been scared to talk to me for years. And now you're threatening to do what?"

"I'm threatening to do exactly what you asked. To show you how a kidnapper would treat you."

I laughed in his face and pushed past him. "I'm gonna go keep dancing. I'll see you guys in the morning. Don't bother waiting up for me. Since neither of you will show me what it's like to be taken, I'll find someone else to. God, I'm so wet just thinking about it." It wasn't a lie. I was starting to really like the idea of being kidnapped and dominated. There was a reason I was wearing a leash tonight. I made it two steps before I felt a strong hand on my neck. Ghost yanked me backwards and spun me around so that I was looked up into his furious eyes.

"I warned you."

I gasped as he shoved me to my knees. I loved when he was rough with me. My jaw dropped when he unzipped his pants. His cock was magnificent. Definitely the biggest I'd ever seen. Although my boyfriend and the hot jocks hadn't exactly set the bar very high. But whatevs. I was working my way up in the world. Soon I'd be gagging on 10" cocks on the regular.

"Ghost," said Teddybear. "What the fuck are you doing?"

"I'm teaching her a lesson. This little slut has been torturing us for years."

I licked my lips. Every dirty word that fell from his mouth made me wetter and wetter. I couldn't wait to feel him inside of me.

"And now that she's turned 18, it's time we showed her how the real world works." Ghost looked down at me. "Suck my cock. Now."

I bit my lip and stared up at him. "Make me."

He grabbed the back of my head and pulled my mouth to his cock. I opened wide and happily took him into my mouth. He didn't hesitate to push me all the way down. And then he kept me there. Which was fine by me. Who needs air when you have a delicious cock in your mouth? Not me.

"Dude, you're gonna choke her," said Teddybear.

"I'll let her breathe in a second. I just needed her to finally shut up for two seconds."

Wow. I knew I annoyed Ghost, but I never realized how much he actually hated me. Oh well. By the end of tonight, he was going to be head over heels in love with me. That was the power of a good blowjob. And I was a pro.

I grabbed his delicious little ass and pushed his cock further down my throat. And for good measure, I hummed a little bit.

"Oh fuck," he muttered.

"I can't be part of this," said Teddybear. He turned to leave.

Damn it! He couldn't leave! That would ruin everything.

I pulled back from Ghost's cock. "Are you really gonna let Teddybear leave? You know he's just gonna go tell Daddy and get you fired. He's wanted the position of head bodyguard ever since he got hired."

Ghost narrowed his eyes at me. And then he looked at Teddybear. "Get back here," he said.

"Why?" asked Teddybear.

"Because she's right. The only way I can be sure that you won't rat me out is if you're guilty too. Don't pretend like you don't wanna fuck her."

"What I want doesn't matter. We're supposed to be protecting her. Not fucking her."

I flashed him a seductive smile as my fingers wandered down my stomach. I didn't stop when I reached my panties. I let my fingers drift lower, circling my wetness. I moaned, but it wasn't just for show. I don't think I'd ever been this horny in my life. I wanted him to fuck me. I wanted both of them to fuck me.

Teddybear's Adam's apple rose and then fell.

"Take your cock out right now, soldier," Ghost said. "That's an order."

Hot damn. I loved when a man took control like that. And I loved it even more when Teddybear dropped his pants. He wasn't quite as long as Ghost, but he was a little thicker.

"Oh my God," I said. "Do all kidnappers have such big cocks?"

Ghost grabbed my leash and led me over to Teddybear. "Suck his cock. Now."

I happily obliged. I gave him my full attention for a few seconds before reaching out and stroking Ghost. It was a shame there were only two of them. I would have loved to stroke a third. And gotten fucked by another…

I pulled back and looked up at my bodyguards. "So is it just the two of you? Or do you have more accomplices? I feel like four kidnappers could *really* teach me a lesson. I've been a very naughty girl."

"Did I say you could talk?" asked Ghost.

I was about to shake my head and go back to sucking cock like a good girl, but then I realized that we were in a spot that wasn't viewable from the closet. *Shit!* "You didn't say I could talk, but I don't really care what you say." I stood up and walked towards the bed.

Ghost caught me halfway there. With his rough hand on my neck, he bent me over. And then he tore off my panties. Seriously. *Tore them off.* My boyfriend always removed them so delicately before we were gonna fuck. But this was so much better. I was instantly soaked.

I expected to feel his cock, but instead he traced his hands down my ass and buried his face in my pussy. He knew exactly where to find my clit. And he sucked on it. Hard.

Fuck yes. I arched my back to give him better access, and he took full advantage of it. His tongue slid into me.

Yeah, I was done fucking around with college guys. This was a million times better. And they hadn't even fucked me yet! Speaking of they, I'd almost forgotten all about Teddybear. But he'd jumped up on the bed and had his cock near my face. So while Ghost ate my pussy like a pro, I gave Teddybear the best blowjob of his life.

Every stroke of Ghost's tongue, every brush of his nose against my clit, every suck…it was all perfect. I was so close to the edge…

But then Ghost stopped.

I pulled back from Teddybear. "No! Don't stop." I was seconds away from coming. I needed it. I needed his tongue back.

"Are you gonna come?" asked Ghost.

"Mhm."

"No you aren't. Not without my permission."

"But…"

He smacked my ass. "No talking."

Fuck, how could I possibly get any wetter?

"Your mouth has one purpose and one purpose only. And that's to suck Teddybear's cock while I fuck your tight little pussy." He grabbed my hips and slammed his cock into me.

Holy shit. Holy fucking shit. I'd never felt something so amazing in my entire life. The size, the veins, the bare skin. *Wait.* Bare skin? *Oh my God.* He wasn't using a condom. And in that moment, I realized I'd never be able to use a condom again. Being rawdogged was literally everything. Especially when I had a nice big cock to suck on at the same time.

I rocked back and forth between the two studs as they used my holes for their pleasure.

I'd always wondered what heaven was like. Now I knew. Heaven was getting double-teamed by two big cocks. I'd fantasized about this countless times. Honestly I'd fantasized about it with both of them countless times. But the real thing was so much better. I felt so…full. So used. So ready to explode.

I could have done it for hours, but a knock on the door ended it way too soon.

"Chastity!" called Topher from out in the hallway. "I got the fireworks!"

"Who the fuck is that?" hissed Ghost.

I reluctantly unwrapped my lips from Teddybear's cock. "Hot Jock #1."

"We're busy," yelled Ghost.

"Chastity?" asked Topher. "Who's in there with you?"

Ghost put his finger to his lips.

"Chastity?!" Topher called again. He started banging on the door.

"Tell him to go away," said Ghost.

"I'll be out soon!" I called. Hopefully not that soon, though. I wanted this to go on forever.

"Who was that guy?" demanded Topher.

"Just my bodyguard."

"Are you okay?"

"She's fine!" yelled Ghost.

"Chastity, I need to see you to make sure you're okay."

"Can you please make this asshole go away?" whispered Ghost. "I'm not done with you yet." He pulled out of me and pushed me towards the door.

I cracked it open - it wouldn't do to have Topher see my two nude bodyguards standing by the bed - and smiled at him. "Hey man, you got the fireworks?"

"Yeah. I found some over…" He paused and his eyes went to my tits.

Oh shit. At some point while I'd been getting railed, one of my bodyguards must have torn my bra off. Because my tits were definitely out.

"Why are you naked with your bodyguards?"

"I spilled something on my dress. They brought me a change of…" A thick cock slid into me mid-sentence. "Clothes," I moaned. Yeah, I was definitely addicted to bare cock now. I couldn't imagine it any other way. I almost orgasmed when he pressed inside of me.

"Are you okay?" asked Topher. He craned his neck to try to look into the room, but the door was only cracked open enough for him to see my face and my naked right boob.

"Yeah. Fine!" I yelled as the guy fucked me harder. It felt a little different than before, so I assumed it was Teddybear. For such a cute name, he fucked me surprisingly hard. His fingers dug into my hips and I had to stifle another moan.

"You're acting weird."

"I get a little loopy when I'm drunk. Go set the fireworks off. I'll watch out the window."

"What about Ash? Is she watching too?"

"Yup," I said and slammed the door shut. Then I turned to look at the man fucking me. As predicted, it was Teddybear.

"You're so bad," I said. "What would my date have thought if he knew I was getting fucked while talking to him?"

"I thought you'd like the thrill of it."

"Well you were wrong. I didn't like it. I fucking loved it." I pushed back onto him until he was balls-deep inside of me, pressing against me in all the right places. *Jesus.*

Ghost grabbed my leash and yanked my head down towards his cock. *Yum.*

Everything up to that moment had been amazing, but now it was ON. My bodyguards fucked me in every corner of the dean's bedroom. They pushed me up against the bedposts. Took me on all fours. Bent me over the loveseat. I was close to the edge, but when Ghost grabbed my hips and lifted me entirely off the ground, I finally shattered. It felt like I was fucking flying as I pulsed around him.

"You weren't allowed to come," growled Ghost. But then he groaned as I clenched down harder around his cock.

Fuck that felt amazing. I shrugged like that wasn't the best orgasm of my life and kept sucking Teddy-bear.

"I'm gonna have to punish you for that. On your knees." He pulled out of me and shoved me to the ground.

Yes, please. I opened wide as they both stroked their cocks a few inches from my face, one on each side. I was about to get caught in the crossfire, and I couldn't freaking wait. I rubbed my aching pussy with one hand and squeezed my tits with the other. Being kidnapped was the fucking best thing ever. I wanted to do it every weekend.

I heard Topher's fireworks going off and turned to look out the window at them, but just then Ghost blew his load right in my face. I closed my eyes *just* in time as his warm cum covered my face. Teddy-bear groaned and added to the mess. The sticky, delicious mess.

Yum.

I made sure they covered me in every last drop. My skin always glowed the most after a good facial.

Chapter 7

TOODLES
Saturday - Sept 7, 2013

"So that's what it's like to be kidnapped, huh?" I asked as I wiped some cum off my cheek and licked it off my finger.

"Yes," said Ghost.

"Well damn. I would have tried to get kidnapped a lot sooner if I'd known it felt that good."

He shook his head. "You're crazy."

"Maybe so. But you didn't seem to mind my craziness when I was gagging on your cock."

He narrowed his eyes. "That was only to teach you a lesson. I took no joy from that."

"Mhm. Suuuure."

"I didn't," he said, but I could have sworn there was a hint of happiness in his voice. The stoic Ghost had finally warmed up to me! This was my chance.

"Well, maybe you'll let yourself enjoy it a little more next time."

"There won't be a next time."

"You sure? Because I was thinking maybe we could come to a little arrangement. You let me go to parties, and I'll let you two use me as your little fuck toy whenever you want."

Ghost stared at me. "Get dressed."

"Is that a yes?" This was actually way better than my Seduction Blackmail plan. Two huge cocks waiting for me at all times sounded like a dream.

"No. This isn't a fucking game, Chastity. You're in danger. And it's my job to protect you."

Wrong choice, bud.

***

I woke up sore in all the right places. *Best. Night. Ever.* I smiled to myself and rolled out of bed, being careful not to wake Ash. I was honestly a little surprised to even see her in the dorm. I thought she would have spent the night with a boy after watching all that sexiness from the closet.

I tiptoed over and grabbed her phone from her nightstand. I nearly squealed with delight when I opened up her gallery.

Score!

I plugged her phone into my computer and got to work. Then I texted my bodyguards and told them I needed their help.

"What do you need?" asked Teddybear. Ghost was back to his usual grumpy self, just standing and glaring at me.

"Well I was working on editing this video, and I can't decide which clip I like most." I spun my laptop around for them to see.

Both of their jaws dropped.

"This clip of you two railing me on the bed is pretty great..." I fast-forwarded a little. "But there's just something so poetic about the fireworks going off in the window behind us as you guys drench me in your cum. Which do you think would make Daddy more likely to kill you?"

"Ahhhh!" screamed Ash.

"What's wrong?" I asked. "Are these oafs scaring you again? Don't worry, bestie. I own them now."

Ash pointed at my screen. "What is..."

I stared at her. "You know this is the footage you took, right?"

"That was on my phone?! Oh my God, I'm going to get arrested."

"I'm so confused. You were in the closet that whole time, right?"

"Yes. But I must have fallen asleep. It was so warm and comfy snuggled up in all those expensive suits."

"Don't worry. You can watch the whole thing back later in private. It's super hot." I winked at her.

Ghost snatched my computer off my desk and hovered his finger over the delete key.

"Go ahead and delete it," I said. "I have backups. And backups of those backups. There's nothing you can do - I own you."

"You wouldn't dare let your precious *Daddy* see you like this."

I raised an eyebrow. "Do you really want to gamble your life on that?"

He stared at me for a long tense moment. And then he put my computer back on my desk. "Fuck you."

"You already did that. I hope it was worth it."

"It was," said Teddybear.

"Shut up!" spat Ghost.

"Now, now, little Ghosty. Please watch your mouth."

"Or what? You'll show your father the tape and get me killed?"

I smiled. "Exactly! Now we're getting somewhere. So here's how this is going to work. I own you now. You'll do whatever I say, when I say it. If I want food, you'll get it. If I need a ride somewhere, you'll drive me. If I'm horny, you'll fuck me. Got it?"

"Yes, ma'am," said Teddybear.

"Good boy. What about you, Ghosty? Do you understand?"

"I'll take the other deal. The one where we let you go to parties."

"Hmmm…let me think." I tapped my lips. "No. That was a one time offer. Should have taken it when you could. Anyway, I like this deal more. Because I still get to go to parties, but now I also have two servants."

"What are we supposed to tell your father?"

"Tell him that I'm a perfect little angel, of course. Whatever he needs to hear in order to not worry about my safety."

"Fine," said Ghost. "I'll play your little game and be your servant. But you better watch your back. Because I'm going to get that tape back. And when I do, you're gonna pay."

There was a glint in his eye that made it seem like I'd be paying with sexual favors. *Oh, Ghost, don't threaten me with something I want.* Silly boy. "Then let the games begin. But first drive over to Denny's and get me a grand slam breakfast. I'm hungry AF."

Ghost grunted and started to walk out.

"Wait," I said.

Ghost and Teddybear stopped and turned around.

"Three things, Ghost. One - your grumpiness is really messing with my good vibes. From now on, I expect to see a smile on your face. Two - Teddybear is now your superior. And three - Ash owns you both too. So get her a grand slam breakfast too. That's all for now. Toodles!" I blew them a kiss and waved them out the door.

Ash stared at me in disbelief.

"What? Was that okay? I was planning on sending them away for good so that they'd stop bothering you, but then I realized that having two manservants would be so much better. Actually, I'll be honest. I kept them for the dick. Did you see how big they are?" I pointed to my computer screen.

Ash put her hand up to block out my screen. But I could tell she was secretly looking through her fingers and loving it. "Wait a second…you did all that because they made me uncomfortable?"

"Of course, bestie." I pulled the translated Single Girl Rules out from under my pillow and brought them over to Ash. "Rule #1: Boys are replaceable. Friends are forever."

"Whoa…I did not ask you to do that," she said.

"I know. But I had to." I pointed to the first rule again.

"I don't think that's what that means."

"Of course it is! I made it so that my bodyguards will be around less because you didn't like them…hence the replaceable boys part. And you're my best friend. Friends are forever! Boom. Nailed it."

"I think it just meant like…have a girls' night or something."

"No. There are instructions for that in rule #2. We'll get to that next, don't you worry your sweet little head. Because we're single girls." I flipped my hair over my shoulder with all the sass.

Ash just stared at me.

"You have to do it too," I said and nudged her shoulder.

"We're single girls," Ash said and flipped her hair over her shoulder.

"Yeah we are!"

"You're going to make me do all these rules, aren't you?" She either looked horrified or excited. It was hard to tell because I was just so freaking excited.

"Heck yeah! Because we're…"

"Single girls," Ash said with an exaggerated sigh.

"Don't look so glum. Rule #13 is going to make you so happy, I promise."

"Good God, what's rule #13? Please say it doesn't involve two men at a time."

Well it probably will now. I could tell she was asking for it. "You'll just have to wait and see." I swore she looked excited for a second. She was definitely kinkier than she was letting on. We were both going to thoroughly enjoy the Single Girl Rules. This was going to be the most unforgettable four years of our lives ever! Especially with Ash by my side. And even though I wasn't learning anything in my dumb classes, I was definitely learning very valuable life lessons. I like my dicks in twos. And Rule #1: Boys are replaceable. Friends are forever.

Epilogue

BLASPHEMY
Present Day - Saturday - Oct 10, 2026

"Okay, I admit. It was fun to reminisce about that crazy night," said Ash. "Now can we *puh-lease* get back to the wedding?! My dress is officially ruined." She lifted her arms to show off her enormous pit stains.

"Of course we can!"

"Thank God." She grabbed the Russian book from me and started to shove it back onto the shelf.

"Whoa, what's the hurry? We'll get back to the wedding eventually, but we still have to go through the rest of the rules."

"But Rule #1 already took…" She checked her phone and her eyes got huge. "Oh my God! That story took thirty minutes. In ten minutes you're officially going to be late for your wedding. I think I'm going to faint."

"Of course I'm going to be late. Two hours late is appropriate, don't you think? I love my shmoopie poo, but I don't want to look like a desperate loser.

And anyway…Single Girl Rule #1: Boys are replaceable. Friends are forever!"

"No! You stop it! I've had it with these damned rules!"

I gaped at her. "Ashley Gertrude Cooper III. I ought to wash your mouth out with soap. That's blasphemy!"

"That's not my name," she muttered.

"I was only going to tell a few more stories, but now I feel like I need to go through every rule."

"Can we do it after the wedding? I think I might be having a heart attack." She fanned herself.

"Just forget about the wedding and enjoy our final moments together as single girls."

"I'm not single." She flashed her giant ring at me.

"In title, perhaps. But in spirit, we'll always be single girls."

"You might seriously be single forever in both title and spirit if we don't leave for your wedding right this instant."

I shook my head. "Girl, you need to relax. Why don't you just pretend like we're having a good old fashioned girls' night? Oooh! That's a perfect segue for rule #2. Do you remember our first girls' night?! That night was literally everything."

"What are you talking about? It was a disaster."

"No, it was everything. EVERYTHING I'm telling you."

Ash folded her arms across her chest. "Don't you do it. Don't you dare launch into another monologue."

"It all started on a dark and stormy girls' night...."

"Stop it!"

"Never! This is one of my all-time favorite stories. I always love the crazy stories."

Ash just stared at me. "You get one more story. So you better make it count." But she was smiling now because we both knew that rule #2 had been totally wild. *Ah, my very first girls' night.* Spoiler alert...Ash and I were both right. It was everything. But it was also a disaster. A hilariously awkward disaster that almost landed us both in jail. And it all started on a dark and stormy girls' night...

What's Next?

Single Girl Rules Book 2 is coming soon! You heard Chastity…she still needs to send these rules off in style before her big wedding!

But while you wait, you can get your very own Single Girl Rules membership card! And some to share with your friends.

SINGLE GIRL RULES
Official Member

1. Boys are replaceable. Friends are forever.
2. Girls' night is every Friday. No exceptions.
3. Never let a friend go into a bathroom alone.
4. You can never have too many shoes.
5. Have wine in your purse at all times.
6. Always kiss and tell.
7. Pics or it didn't happen.
8. If a man has 8 abs and 8 inches, he may not be refused.
9. If you hear about a well-hung man, share the news.
10. All celebrations of important life events must involve strippers.

For your printable membership cards, go to:
www.ivysmoak.com/sgr1-pb

The Society

#STALKERPROBLEMS

You know that Chastity is going to get her man (or men…), but what about poor, sweet Ash?

Well I have some good news… Ash has an entire series all about her wild journey to find love! And you better believe Chastity is gonna be there every step of the way to help her.

And yes, Ash is definitely going to still be abiding by the Single Girl Rules. In fact, in the Society, you'll learn about at least 10 more of the rules.

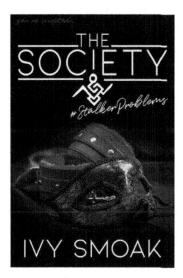

I got an invitation to an illicit club.

They say they'll grant me three wishes.

They say they'll make all my wildest dreams come true.

All I have to do is sign the contract.

Is it too good to be true? I'm about to find out.

Get your copy today!

A Note From Ivy

The Single Girl Rules are my new happy place. Chastity and Ash always make me laugh so hard and I hope they had you laughing too.

This is basically the college experience of my dreams. I was super shy and reserved like Ash and boy could I have used a Chastity in my life! And the Single Girl Rules. I think we could all learn a thing or two from them.

There's just one problem…you don't know all the rules yet! So I hope you loved this first novella. Because spoiler alert – there are a bunch more coming. Girl, there are a ton of rules! Each one more epic than the last.

So pop a squat and get ready for the wildest ride ever. You've started this crazy journey, so you're automatically a card-carrying member of the Single Girl Rules. I don't care if you're single or not. It just happened. We're all doing this together!

And help a fellow single girl out – who here has a TikTok? #BookTok is freaking HUGE right now. So let's make the Single Girl Rules go viral together!!! I'd love to hear you quoting, acting out, or doing anything you can imagine with your favorite #SingleGirlRules on TikTok! Channel your inner Chastity and bring the sass. Let's break #BookTok

together! And don't forget to follow and tag me
@ivysmoak :)

Ivy Smoak
Wilmington, DE
www.ivysmoak.com

About the Author

Ivy Smoak is the Wall Street Journal, USA Today, and Amazon #1 bestselling author of *The Hunted Series*. Her books have sold over 2 million copies worldwide.

When she's not writing, you can find Ivy binge watching too many TV shows, taking long walks, playing outside, and generally refusing to act like an adult. She lives with her husband in Delaware.

Facebook: IvySmoakAuthor
Instagram: @IvySmoakAuthor
Goodreads: IvySmoak